THE SEVEN VOYAGES OF SINDBAD THE SAILOR

GOLU KUMAR

Contents

ONE

A lowly porter by the name of Sindbad resided in Bagdad during the reign of Caliph Haroun-al-Raschid. On a particularly hot day, he was tasked with transporting a large load from one end of the city to the other. He found himself on a quiet street where the pavement was dusted with rose water and a cool breeze was blowing. Before he had even traveled half the distance, he was so exhausted that he placed his load down and sat down to rest in the shade of a large home. He quickly realized that he could not have made a better choice of location because the open windows were emitting a mouthwatering aroma of aloe wood and pastilles, which blended with the rose water scent that was steaming up from the scorching pavement.
He detected some music inside the palace, as well as the lilting cries of nightingales and other birds, and he deduced that feasting and revelry were taking place based on these sounds and the enticing aroma of numerous delicate delicacies.

Because he had never seen this wonderful mansion before and rarely had reason to travel by the block where it was located, he wondered who lived there. He approached some elegantly dressed servants who were stationed at the door and inquired of one of them who the owner of the mansion was.

What, he asked, "do you live in Bagdad and not know that the noble Sindbad the Sailor, that illustrious traveler who traversed every sea where the sun shone, resides here?"

The porter, who had frequently overheard people discussing Sindbad's enormous wealth, could not help but feel jealous of someone whose lot appeared to be as happy as his own was unhappy. He looked up into the sky and said out loud,

"Think about the disparities between Sindbad's life and mine, Mighty Creator of all things. While the fortunate Sindbad spends money left and right and subsists on the fat of the land, I daily endure a thousand hardships and calamities and labor extremely hard just to get by and provide for my family! What has he done to deserve this good life, and what have I done to deserve such a harsh fate?"

Saying this, he stomped on the ground like a miserable and hopeless person. A servant appeared outside the palace at this very moment and grabbed the man by the arm, saying, "Come with me, the noble Sindbad, my master, desires to talk to you."

Sindbad attempted to make an apology by claiming that he was unable to leave the load that had been placed on him in the street since he was not the least bit shocked by the call and worried that his careless comments would have aroused Sindbad's wrath. However, the lackey assured him that it would be taken care of and compelled him to answer the call so forcefully that the porter was finally forced to comply.

He followed the servant into a vast room, where a great company was seated around a table covered with all sorts of delicacies. In the place of honor sat a tall, grave man whose long white beard gave him a venerable air. Behind his chair stood a crowd of attendants eager to minister to his wants. This was the famous Sindbad himself. The porter, more than ever alarmed at the sight of so much magnificence, tremblingly saluted the noble company. Sindbad, making a sign to him to approach, caused him to be seated at his right hand, and himself heaped choice morsels upon his plate and poured out for him a draught of excellent wine, and presently, when the banquet drew to a close, spoke to him familiarly, asking his name and occupation.

I'm called Hindbad, the porter retorted, "My lord."

Sindbad added, "I am pleased to see you here. And I will speak for the group as a whole when I say that everyone is content, but I do need you to clarify what you stated earlier in the street. Because Sindbad sent for him after hearing his complaint while passing by the open window before the feast started.

Sindbad was completely perplexed by the inquiry and responded, "My Lord, I confess that overtaken by fatigue and ill-humor, I uttered indiscreet words, which I beseech you to pardon me," with his head down low.

"Oh!" replied Sindbad, "do not imagine that I am so unjust as to blame you. On the contrary, I understand your situation and can pity you. Only you appear to be mistaken about me, and I wish to set you right. You doubtless imagine that I have acquired all the wealth and luxury you see me enjoy without difficulty or danger, but this is far from being the case. I have only reached this happy state after having suffered every possible kind of toil and danger for years.

"Yes, my noble friends," he continued, addressing the company, "I assure you that my adventures have been strange enough to deter even the most avaricious men from seeking wealth by traversing the seas. Since you have, perhaps, heard but confused accounts of my seven voyages, and the dangers and wonders that I have met with by sea and land, I will now give you a full and true account of them, which I think you will be well pleased to hear."

Before starting his story, Sindbad gave the order to have the load that had been left in the street carried by some of his servants to the location that Hindbad had initially set out for, while he stayed to listen to the tale. This was because the porter played a significant role in Sindbad's adventures.

Initial Voyage

I had inherited a sizeable amount of money from my parents, and because I was young and foolish, I initially wasted it on every kind of pleasure. However, over time, I realized that if wealth is managed poorly, as mine was, and that being old and poor is indeed miserable, I started to consider how I could make the most of what was still left to me.

I joined a group of seafaring merchants after having all of my possessions sold at a public auction. We set off from Balsora on a ship that we had jointly outfitted.

We set sail and took our course towards the East Indies by the Persian Gulf, having the coast of Persia upon our left hand and upon our right the shores of Arabia Felix. I was at first much troubled by the uneasy motion of the vessel, but speedily recovered my health, and since that hour has been no more plagued by sea sickness.

From time to time we landed at various islands, where we sold or exchanged our merchandise, and one day, when the wind dropped suddenly, we found ourselves becalmed close to a small island like a green meadow, which only rose slightly above the surface of the water. Our sails were furled, and the captain permitted all who wished to land for a while and amuse themselves. I was among the number, but when after strolling about for some time we lighted a fire and sat down to enjoy the repast which we had brought with us, we were startled by a sudden and violent trembling of the island, while at the same moment those left upon the ship set up an outcry bidding us come on board for our lives since what we had taken for an island was nothing but the back of a sleeping whale. Those who were nearest to the boat threw themselves into it, others sprang into the sea, but before I could save myself the whale plunged suddenly into the depths of the ocean, leaving me clinging to a piece of the wood that we had brought to make our fire. Meanwhile, a breeze had sprung up, and in the confusion that ensued on board our vessel in hoisting the sails and taking up those who were in the boat and clinging to its sides, no one missed me and I was left at the mercy of the waves. All that day I floated up and down, now beaten this way, now that, and when night fell I despaired for my life; but, weary and spent as I was, I clung to my frail support, and great was my joy when the morning light showed me that I had drifted against an island.

The cliffs were high and steep, but luckily for me some tree roots protruded in places, and by their aid, I climbed up at last and stretched myself upon the turf at the top, where I lay, more dead than alive, till the sun was high in the heavens. By that time I was very hungry, but after some searching, I came upon some eatable herbs, and a spring of clear water, and much refreshed I set out to explore the island. Presently I reached a great plain where a grazing horse was tethered, and as I stood looking at it I heard voices talking underground, and in a moment a man appeared who asked me how I came upon the island. I told him my adventures and heard in return that he was one of the grooms of Mirage, the king of the island and that each year they came to feed their master's horses in this plain. He took me to a cave where his companions were assembled, and when I had eaten of the food they set before me, they bade me think myself fortunate to have come upon them when I did, since they were going back to their master on the morrow, and without their aid, I could certainly never have found my way to the inhabited part of the island.

Early the next morning we accordingly set out, and when we reached the capital I was graciously received by the king, to whom I related my adventures, upon which he ordered that I should be well cared for and provided with such things as I needed. Being a merchant I sought out men of my profession, and particularly those who came from foreign countries, as I hoped in this way to hear news from Bagdad, and find out some means of returning thither, for the capital was situated upon the sea-shore and visited by vessels from all parts of the world. In the meantime, I heard many curious things, and answered many questions concerning my own country, for I talked willingly with all who came to me. Also to while away the time of waiting I explored a little island named Cassel, which belonged to King Mirage, and was supposed to be inhabited by a spirit named Denial. Indeed, the sailors assured me that often at night the playing of timbals could be heard upon it. However, I saw nothing strange upon my voyage, saving some fish that were full two hundred cubits long, but were, fortunately, more in dread of us than even we were of them, and fled from us if we did but strike upon a board to frighten them. Other fishes there were only a cubit long which had heads like owls.

One day after my return, as I went down to the quay, I saw a ship that had just cast anchor and was discharging her cargo, while the merchants to whom it belonged were busily directing the removal of it to their warehouses. Drawing nearer I presently noticed that my name was marked upon some of the packages, and after having carefully examined them, I felt sure that they were indeed those which I had put on board our ship at Balsora. I then recognized the captain of the vessel, but as I was certain that he believed me to be dead, I went up to him and asked who owned the packages that I was looking at.

"There was on board my ship," he replied, "a merchant of Bagdad named Sindbad. One day he and several of my other passengers landed upon what we supposed to be an island, but which was an enormous whale floating asleep upon the waves. No sooner did it feel upon its back the heat of the fire which had been kindled, than it plunged into the depths of the sea. Several of the people who were upon it perished in the waters and among others this unlucky Sindbad. This merchandise is his, but I have resolved to dispose of it for the benefit of his family if I should ever chance to meet with them."

"Captain," said I, "I am that Sindbad whom you believe to be dead, and these are my possessions!"

The captain was shocked when he heard these comments, "What has the world come to, Lackaday? Nowadays, it is difficult to meet an honest man. Did I not watch Sindbad drown with my own eyes, and now you have the gall to claim to be him! I would have assumed you to be a just guy, but you are willing to make up this terrible lie to get what doesn't belong to you."

I requested that you be patient and listen to my narrative.

The captain retorted, "Speak then; I'm all attention."

So I told him of my escape and of my fortunate meeting with the king's grooms, and how kindly I had been received at the palace. Very soon I began to see that I had made some impression upon him, and after the arrival of some of the other merchants, who showed great joy at once more seeing me alive, he declared that he also recognized me.

Throwing himself upon my neck he exclaimed, "Heaven be praised that you have escaped from so great a danger. As to your goods, I pray you to take them and dispose of them as you please." I thanked him, and praised his honesty, begging him to accept several bales of merchandise in token of my gratitude, but he would take nothing. Of the choicest of my goods, I prepared a present for King Mirage, who was at first amazed, having known that I had lost my all. However, when I had explained to him how my bales had been miraculously restored to me, he graciously accepted my gifts, and in return gave me many valuable things. I then took leave of him, and exchanging my merchandise for sandal and aloes wood, camphor, nutmegs, cloves, pepper, and ginger, I embarked upon the same vessel and traded so successfully upon our homeward voyage that I arrived in Balsora with about one hundred thousand sequins. My family received me with as much joy as I felt upon seeing them once more. I bought land and slaves and built a great house in which I resolved to live happily and enjoy all the pleasures of life to forget my past sufferings.

Here Sindbad paused, and commanded the musicians to play again, while the feasting continued until evening. When the time came for the porter to depart, Sindbad gave him a purse containing one hundred sequins, saying, "Take this, Hindbad, and go home, but tomorrow come again and you shall hear more of my adventures."

You can imagine that the porter was well received at home, where his wife and kids thanked their lucky stars that he had met such a donor before he retired very overcome by such generosity.

The following day, Hindbad returned to the traveler's home prepared to impress and was welcomed with open arms. The meal started as soon as all of the guests came, and after they had feasted for a while and were having a good time, Sindbad addressed them as follows:

My friends, I humbly request that you pay attention while I recount the events of my second expedition, which you will find to be even more amazing than the first.

Following Voyage

As you are aware, I decided to retire to Bagdad after my first voyage. However, after a short while, I grew bored with such a sedentary existence and yearned to set sail once more.

I procured, therefore, such goods as were suitable for the places I intended to visit, and embarked for the second time on a good ship with other merchants whom I knew to be honorable men. We went from island to island, often making excellent bargains, until one day we landed at a spot which, though covered with fruit trees and abounding in springs of excellent water, appeared to possess neither houses nor people. While my companions wandered here and there gathering flowers and fruit I sat down in a shady place, and, having heartily enjoyed the provisions and the wine I had brought with me, I fell asleep, lulled by the murmur of a clear brook which flowed close by.

How long I slept I know not, but when I opened my eyes and started to my feet I perceived with horror that I was alone and that the ship was gone. I rushed to and fro like one distracted, uttering cries of despair, and when from the shore I saw the vessel under full sail just disappearing upon the horizon, I wished bitterly enough that I had been content to stay at home in safety. But since wishes could do me no good, I presently took courage and looked about me for a means of escape. When I had climbed a tall tree I, first of all, directed my anxious glances towards the sea; but, finding nothing hopeful there, I turned landward, and my curiosity was excited by a huge dazzling white object, so far off that I could not make out what it might be.

Descending from the tree I hastily collected what remained of my provisions and set off as fast as I could go towards it. As I drew near it seemed to me to be a white ball of immense size and height, and when I could touch it, I found it marvelously smooth and soft. As it was impossible to climb it--for it presented no foot-hold--I walked round about it seeking some opening, but there was none. I counted, however, that it was at least fifty paces round. By this time the sun was near setting, but quite suddenly it fell dark, something like a huge black cloud came swiftly over me, and I saw with amazement that it was a bird of extraordinary size which was hovering near. Then I remembered that I had often heard the sailors speak of a wonderful bird called a roc, and it occurred to me that the white object which had so puzzled me must be its egg.

Sure enough, the bird settled slowly down upon it, covering it with its wings to keep it warm, and I cowered close beside the egg in such a position that one of the bird's feet, which was as large as the trunk of a tree, was just in front of me. Taking off my turban I bound myself securely to it with the linen in the hope that the roc when it took flight the next morning, would bear me away with it from the desolate island. And this was precisely what did happen. As soon as the dawn appeared the bird rose into the air carrying me up and up till I could no longer see the earth, and then suddenly it descended so swiftly that I almost lost consciousness. When I became aware that the roc had settled and that I was once again upon solid ground, I hastily unbound my turban from its foot and freed myself, and that not a moment too soon; for the bird, pouncing upon a huge snake, killed it with a few blows from its powerful beak, and seizing it up rose into the air once more and soon disappeared from my view. When I had looked about me I began to doubt if I had gained anything by quitting the desolate island.

The valley in which I found myself was deep and narrow, and surrounded by mountains that towered into the clouds, and were so steep and rocky that there was no way of climbing up their sides. As I wandered about, seeking anxiously some means of escaping from this trap, I observed that the ground was strewed with diamonds, some of them of an astonishing size. This sight gave me great pleasure, but my delight was speedily damped when I saw also numbers of horrible snakes so long and so large that the smallest of them could have swallowed an elephant with ease. Fortunately for me, they seemed to hide in caverns of the rocks by day and only came out by night, probably because of their enemy the roc.

All day long I wandered up and down the valley, and when it grew dusk I crept into a little cave and blocked up the entrance to it with a stone, I ate part of my little store of food and lay down to sleep, but all through the night, the serpents crawled to and fro, hissing horribly so that I could scarcely close my eyes for terror. I was thankful when the morning light appeared, and when I judged by the silence that the serpents had retreated to their dens I came tremblingly out of my cave and wandered up and down the valley once more, kicking the diamonds contemptuously out of my path, for I felt that they were indeed vain things to a man in my situation. At last, overcome with weariness, I sat down upon a rock, but I had hardly closed my eyes when I was startled by something which fell to the ground with a thud close beside me.

It was a huge piece of fresh meat, and as I stared at it several more pieces rolled over the cliffs in different places. I had always thought that the stories the sailors told of the famous valley of diamonds, and of the cunning way which some merchants had devised for getting at the precious stones, were mere travelers' tales invented to give pleasure to the hearers, but now I perceived that they were surely true. These merchants came to the valley at the time when the eagles, which keep their eyries in the rocks, had hatched they're young. The merchants then threw great lumps of meat into the valley. These, falling with so much force upon the diamonds, were sure to take up some of the precious stones with them, when the eagles pounced upon the meat and carried it off to their nests to feed their hungry broods. Then the merchants, scaring away the parent birds with shouts and outcries, would secure their treasures. Until this moment I had looked upon the valley as my grave, for I had seen no possibility of getting out of it alive, but now I took courage and began to devise a means of escape. I began by picking up all the largest diamonds I could find and storing them carefully in the leathern wallet which had held my provisions; this I tied securely to my belt. I then chose the piece of meat which seemed most suited to my purpose, and with the aid of my turban bound it firmly to my back; this done I laid down upon my face and awaited the coming of the eagles. I soon heard the flapping of their mighty wings above me, and had the satisfaction of feeling one of them seize upon my piece of meat, and me with it, and rise slowly towards his nest, into which he presently dropped me. Luckily for me, the merchants were on the watch, and setting up their usual outcries they rushed to the nest scaring away the eagle. Their amazement was great when they discovered me, and also their disappointment, and with one accord they fell to abusing me for having robbed them of their usual profit. Addressing myself to the one who seemed most aggrieved, I said: "I am sure, if you knew all that I have suffered, you would show more kindness towards me, and as for diamonds, I have enough here of the very best for you and me and all your company." So saying I showed them to him. The others all crowded around me, wondering at my adventures and admiring the device by which I had escaped from the valley, and when they had led me to their camp and examined my diamonds, they assured me that in all the years that they had carried on their trade they had seen no stones to be compared with them for size and beauty.

I found that each merchant chose a particular nest, and took his chance on what he might find in it. So I begged the one who owned the nest to which I had been carried to take as much as he would of my treasure, but he contented himself with one stone, and that by no means the largest, assuring me that with such a gem his fortune was made, and he need toil no more. I stayed with the merchants several days, and then as they were journeying homewards I gladly accompanied them. Our way lay across high mountains infested with frightful serpents, but we had the good luck to escape them and came at last to the seashore. Thence we sailed to the isle of Rohat where the camphor trees grow to such a size that a hundred men could shelter under one of them with ease. The sap flows from an incision made high up in the tree into a vessel hung there to receive it, and soon hardens into the substance called camphor, but the tree itself withers up and dies when it has been so treated.

On this same island, we saw the rhinoceros, an animal that is smaller than the elephant and larger than the buffalo. It has one horn about a cubit long which is solid but has a furrow from the base to the tip. Upon it is traced in white lines the figure of a man. The rhinoceros fights with the elephant, and transfixing him with his horn carries him off upon his head, but becoming blinded with the blood of his enemy, he falls helpless to the ground, and then comes the roc, and clutches them both up in his talons and takes them to feed his young. This doubtless astonishes you, but if you do not believe my tale go to Rohat and see for yourself. For fear of wearying you I pass over in silence many other wonderful things which we saw on this island. Before we left I exchanged one of my diamonds for much goodly merchandise by which I profited greatly on our homeward way. At last, we reached Balsora, whence I hastened to Bagdad, where my first action was to bestow large sums of money upon the poor, after which I settled down to enjoy the tranquility the riches I had gained with so much toil and pain.

After recounting the events of his second voyage, Sindbad again gave Hindbad 100 sequins and invited him to return the following day to hear about his third voyage's experiences. The other visitors left as well to return to their homes, but everyone arrived back at the same time the following day, including the porter, whose previous life of hardship had already started to feel like a nightmare to him. Sindbad once more demanded the attention of his companions when the meal was finished and started to describe his third adventure.

Voyage No. 3

My two journeys' dangers were quickly forgotten by me thanks to the nice, carefree life I was leading. Furthermore, since I was still in my prime, being active thrilled me more. Having once more stocked up on Bagdad's most exclusive and luxurious goods, I then transported them to Balsora before setting out for foreign shores with other merchants I know. We had visited a lot of ports and were making a lot of money when, one day, on the open sea, we were caught in a horrible storm that completely blew us off course. The wind lasted for many days before forcing us to anchor on a remote island.

"I would rather have come to anchor anywhere than here," quoth our captain. "This island and all adjoining it are inhabited by hairy savages, who are certain to attack us, and whatever these dwarfs may do we dare not resist, since they swarm like locusts, and if one of them is killed the rest will fall upon us, and speedily make an end of us."

These words caused great consternation among all the ship's company, and only too soon we were to find out that the captain spoke truly. There appeared a vast multitude of hideous savages, not more than two feet high and covered with reddish fur. Throwing themselves into the waves they surrounded our vessel. Chattering meanwhile in a language we could not understand, and clutching at ropes and gangways, they swarmed up the ship's side with such speed and agility that they almost seemed to fly.

You may imagine the rage and terror that seized us as we watched them, neither daring to hinder them nor able to speak a word to deter them from their purpose, whatever it might be. Of this, we were not left long in doubt. Hoisting the sails, and cutting the cable of the anchor, they sailed our vessel to an island which lay a little further off, where they drove us ashore; then taking possession of her, they made off to the place from which they had come, leaving us helpless upon a shore avoided with horror by all mariners for a reason which you will soon learn.

Turning away from the sea we wandered miserably inland, finding as we went various herbs and fruits which we ate, feeling that we might as well live as long as possible though we had no hope of escape. Presently we saw in the far distance what seemed to us to be a splendid palace, towards which we turned our weary steps, but when we reached it we saw that it was a castle, lofty, and strongly built. Pushing back the heavy ebony doors we entered the courtyard, but upon the threshold of the great hall beyond it, we paused, frozen with horror, at the sight which greeted us. On one side lay a huge pile of bones--human bones, and on the other numberless spits for roasting! Overcome with despair we sank trembling to the ground and lay there without speech or motion. The sun was setting when a loud noise aroused us, the door of the hall violently burst open and a horrible giant entered. He was as tall as a palm tree, perfectly black, and had one eye, which flamed like a burning coal in the middle of his forehead. His teeth were long and sharp and grinned, while his lower lip hung down upon his chest, and he had ears like elephant's ears, which covered his shoulders, and nails like the claws of some fierce bird.

At this terrible sight, our senses left us and we lay like dead men. When at last we came to ourselves the giant sat examining us attentively with his fearful eye. Presently when he had looked at us enough he came towards us, and stretching out his hand took me by the back of the neck, turning me this way and that, but feeling that I was mere skin and bone he set me down again and went on to the next, whom he treated in the same fashion; at last, he came to the captain, and finding him the fattest of us all, he took him up in one hand and stuck him upon a spit and proceeded to kindle a huge fire at which he presently roasted him. After the giant had supped he lay down to sleep, snoring like the loudest thunder, while we lay shivering with horror the whole night through, and when day broke he awoke and went out, leaving us in the castle.

When we believed him to be gone we started bemoaning our horrible fate, until the hall echoed with our despairing cries. Though we were many and our enemy was alone it did not occur to us to kill him, and indeed we should have found that a hard task, even if we had thought of it, and no plan could we devise to deliver ourselves. So at last, submitting to our sad fate, we spent the day wandering up and down the island eating such fruits as we could find, and when night came we returned to the castle, having sought in vain for any other place of shelter. At sunset, the giant returned, supped upon one of our unhappy comrades, slept and snored till dawn, and then left us as before. Our condition seemed to us so frightful that several of my companions thought it would be better to leap from the cliffs and perish in the waves at once, rather than await so miserable an end; but I had a plan of escape which I now unfolded to them, and which they at once agreed to attempt.

"Listen, my brothers," I added. "You know that plenty of driftwood lies along the shore. Let us make several rafts, and carry them to a suitable place. If our plot succeeds, we can wait patiently for the chance of some passing ship that would rescue us from this fatal island. If it fails, we must quickly take to our rafts; frail as they are, we have more chance of saving our lives with them than we have if we remain here."

All agreed with me, and we spent the day building rafts, each capable of carrying three persons. At nightfall, we returned to the castle, and very soon in came the giant, and one more of our number was sacrificed. But the time of our vengeance was at hand! As soon as he had finished his horrible repast he lay down to sleep as before, and when we heard him begin to snore I, and nine of the boldest of my comrades, rose softly and took each a spit, which we made red-hot in the fire, and then at a given signal, we plunged it with one accord into the giant's eye, completely blinding him. Uttering a terrible cry, he sprang to his feet clutching in all directions to try to seize one of us, but we had all fled different ways as soon as the deed was done, and thrown ourselves flat upon the ground in corners where he was not likely to touch us with his feet.

After a vain search, he fumbled about till he found the door, and fled out of it howling frightfully. As for us, when he was gone we made haste to leave the fatal castle, and, stationing ourselves beside our rafts, we waited to see what would happen. Our idea was that if, when the sun rose, we saw nothing of the giant, and no longer heard his howls, which still came faintly through the darkness, growing more and more distant, we should conclude that he was dead and that we might safely stay upon the island and need not risk our lives upon the frail rafts. But alas! morning light showed us our enemy approaching us, supported on either hand by two giants nearly as large and fearful as himself, while a crowd of others followed close upon their heels. Hesitating no longer we clambered upon our rafts and rowed with all our might out to sea. The giants, seeing their prey escaping them, seized up huge pieces of rock, and wading into the water hurled them after us with the such good aim that all the rafts except the one I was upon were swamped, and their luckless crews drowned, without our being able to do anything to help them. Indeed I and my two companions had all we could do to keep our raft beyond the reach of the giants, but by dint of hard rowing we, at last, gained the open sea. Here we were at the mercy of the winds and waves, which tossed us to and fro all that day and night, but the next morning we found ourselves near an island, upon which we gladly landed.

There we found delicious fruits and having satisfied our hunger we presently lay down to rest upon the shore. Suddenly we were aroused by a loud rustling noise, and starting up, saw that it was caused by an immense snake that was gliding towards us over the sand. So swiftly it came that it had seized one of my comrades before he had time to fly, and despite his cries and struggles speedily crushed the life out of him in its mighty coils and proceeded to swallow him. By this time my other companion and I were running for our lives to some place where we might hope to be safe from this new horror, and seeing a tall tree we climbed up into it, having first provided ourselves with a store of fruit off the surrounding bushes. When night came I fell asleep, but only to be awakened once more by the terrible snake, which after hissing horribly round the tree, at last, reared itself up against it, and finding my sleeping comrade who was perched just below me, it swallowed him also and crawled away leaving me half dead with terror.

When the sun rose I crept down from the tree with hardly a hope of escaping the dreadful fate which had overtaken my comrades, but life is sweet, and I determined to do all I could to save myself. All day long I toiled with frantic haste and collected quantities of dry brushwood, reeds, and thorns, which I bound with faggots, and making a circle of them under my tree I piled them firmly one upon another until I had a kind of tent in which I crouched like a mouse in a hole when she sees the cat coming. You may imagine what a fearful night I passed, for the snake returned eager to devour me, and glided round and round my frail shelter seeking an entrance. Every moment I feared that it would succeed in pushing aside some of the faggots, but happily for me they held together, and when it grew light my enemy retired, baffled and hungry, to his den. As for me, I was dead than alive! Shaking with fright and half suffocated by the poisonous breath of the monster, I came out of my tent and crawled down to the sea, feeling that it would be better to plunge from the cliffs and end my life at once than pass such another night of horror. But to my joy and relief, I saw a ship sailing by, and by shouting wildly and waving my turban I managed to attract the attention of her crew.

A boat was sent to rescue me, and very soon I found myself on board surrounded by a wondering crowd of sailors and merchants eager to know by what chance I found myself on that desolate island. After I had told my story they regaled me with the choicest food the ship afforded, and the captain, seeing that I was in rags, generously bestowed upon me one of his coats. After sailing about for some time and touching at many ports we came at last to the island of Salahat, where sandal wood grows in great abundance. Here we anchored, and as I stood watching the merchants disembarking their goods and preparing to sell or exchange them, the captain came up to me and said,

"I'm holding some goods for a deceased passenger of mine, my brother. When I meet with his heirs, I will be able to give them the money, but it will only be fair that you receive a portion for your trouble. Would you kindly do me the favor of trading with it?"

I happily agreed because I didn't want to see others do anything. Then, after showing me where the bales were, he sent for the person tasked with maintaining a list of the cargo on the ship. When this individual arrived, he inquired as to the name under which the goods should be registered.

The captain retorted, "In the name of Sindbad the Sailor."

Although he had changed significantly since then, I recognized him as the captain of the ship on which I had completed my second cruise after being greatly astonished by his statement. It was understandable why he hadn't recognized me if he thought I was dead.

I responded, "So, captain, the merchant who was the owner of those bales was named Sindbad?"

Yes, he answered. "He had that name. He belonged to Bagdad and joined my ship in Balsora, but due to an accident, he was left behind on a barren island where we had landed to fill up our water cans. It took four hours before he was discovered to be missing. By that point, the wind had picked up, making it hard to put him back."

I responded, "You think he's dead then?"

He replied, "Alas! yeah.

Captain, why? I sobbed "well look at me I am the Sindbad who dozed off on the island and discovered himself abandoned when he awakened."

The captain gave me a startled look but quickly realized that I was telling the truth and was ecstatic about my escape.

At the very least, I'm relieved that act of negligence is no longer on my mind, he added. Take your things and the profit I made off of them, and may you be successful in the future.

I took them gratefully, and as we went from one island to another I laid in stores of cloves, cinnamon, and other spices. In one place I saw a tortoise which was twenty cubits long and as many broad, also a fish that was like a cow and had skin so thick that it was used to make shields. Another I saw was like a camel in shape and color. So by degrees, we came back to Balsora, and I returned to Bagdad with so much money that I could, not myself count it, besides treasures without end. I gave largely to the poor, and bought much land to add to what I already possessed, and thus ended my third voyage.

The next day, once they had all gathered and the meal was over, their host continued his exploits. When Sindbad had done telling his tale, he gave Hindbad another 100 sequins. Sindbad then left with the other guests.

Voyage No. 4

Even though I was wealthy and content after my third trip, I couldn't bring myself to stay at home. I organized my business and started traveling across some of the Persian provinces because I enjoyed dealing with and seeing new and unusual things. Before setting out on my tour, I sent off stockpiles of products to be ready for my arrival in the various locations I wished to visit.

I boarded the ship in a far-off port, and things went smoothly for a while. However, after getting trapped in a fierce hurricane, our ship eventually sank despite our honorable captain's best efforts to salvage her, and many of our companies perished in the seas. The storm had driven us close to an island, and after crawling up above the reach of the waves, we threw ourselves down completely tired to wait for dawn. I, along with a few others, had the good fortune to be swept ashore clinging to fragments of the wreck.

At daylight, we wandered inland, and soon saw some huts, to which we directed our steps. As we drew near their black inhabitants swarmed out in great numbers and surrounded us, and we were led to their houses and were divided among our captors. I with five others was taken into a hut, where we were made to sit upon the ground, and certain herbs were given to us, which the blacks made signs to us to eat. Observing that they did not touch them, I was careful only to pretend to taste my portion; but my companions, being very hungry, rashly ate up all that was set before them, and very soon I had the horror of seeing them become perfectly mad. Though they chattered incessantly I could not understand a word they said, nor did they heed when I spoke to them. The savages now produced large bowls full of rice prepared with cocoanut oil, of which my crazy comrades ate eagerly, but I only tasted a few grains, understanding clearly that the object of our captors was to fatten us speedily for their eating, and this was exactly what happened. My unlucky companions having lost their reason, felt neither anxiety nor fear, and ate greedily all that was offered them. So they were soon fat and there was an end of them, but I grew leaner day by day, for I ate but little, and even that little did me no good because of my fear of what lay before me. However, as I was so far from being a tempting morsel, I was allowed to wander about freely, and one day, when all the blacks had gone off upon some expedition leaving only an old man to guard me, I managed to escape from him and plunged into the forest, running faster the more he cried to me to come back until I had completely distanced him.

For seven days I hurried on, resting only when the darkness stopped me, and living chiefly upon cocoanuts, which afforded me both meat and drink, and on the eighth day, I reached the seashore and saw a party of white men gathering pepper, which grew abundantly all about. Reassured by the nature of their occupation, I advanced towards them and they greeted me in Arabic, asking who I was and whence I came. My delight was great on hearing this familiar speech, and I willingly satisfied their curiosity, telling them how I had been shipwrecked, and captured by the blacks. "But these savages devour men!" said they. "How did you escape?" I repeated to them what I have just told you, at which they were mightily astonished. I stayed with them until they had collected as much pepper as they wished, and then they took me back to their own country and presented me to their king, by whom I was hospitably received. To him also I had to relate my adventures, which surprised him much, and when I had finished he ordered that I should be supplied with food and raiment and treated with consideration.

The island on which I found myself was full of people, and abounded in all sorts of desirable things, and a great deal of traffic went on in the capital, where I soon began to feel at home and contented. Moreover, the king treated me with special favor, and in consequence of this everyone, whether at the court or in the town, sought to make life pleasant for me. One thing I remarked which I thought very strange; was that from the greatest to the least, all men rode their horses without bridle or stirrups. I one day presumed to ask his majesty why he did not use them, to which he replied, "You speak to me of things of which I have never before heard!" This gave me an idea. I found a clever workman and made him cut out under my direction the foundation of a saddle, which I wadded and covered with choice leather, adorning it with rich gold embroidery. I then got a lock-smith to make me a bit and a pair of spurs after a pattern that I drew for him, and when all these things were completed I presented them to the king and showed him how to use them. When I had saddled one of his horses he mounted it and rode about quite delighted with the novelty, and to show his gratitude he rewarded me with large gifts. After this I had to make saddles for all the principal officers of the king's household, and as they all gave me rich presents I soon became very wealthy and quite an important person in the city.

One day the king sent for me and said, "Sindbad, I am going to ask a favor of you. Both I and my subjects esteem you and wish you to end your days amongst us. Therefore I desire that you will marry a rich and beautiful lady whom I will find for you, and think no more of your own country."

As the king's will was law I accepted the charming bride he presented to me, and lived happily with her. Nevertheless, I had every intention of escaping at the first opportunity, and going back to Bagdad. Things were thus going prosperously with me when it happened that the wife of one of my neighbors, with whom I had struck up quite a friendship, fell ill, and presently died. I went to his house to offer my consolations and found him in the depths of woe.

I prayed, "May heaven keep you and grant you a long life!"

But, he added, "What good is saying that when I just have an hour to live? "

"Come, come, surely it's not as horrible as all that, I exclaimed. I hope I can spare you for a very long time."

"I hope," answered he, "that your life may be long, but as for me, all is finished. I have set my house in order, and today I shall be buried with my wife. This has been the law upon our island from the earliest ages--the living husband goes to the grave with his dead wife, the living wife with her dead husband. So did our fathers, and so must we do. The law changes not, and all must submit to it!"

As he spoke the friends and relations of the unhappy pair began to assemble. The body, decked in rich robes and sparkling with jewels, was laid upon an open bier, and the procession started, taking its way to a high mountain at some distance from the city, the wretched husband, clothed from head to foot in a black mantle, following mournfully.

When the place of interment was reached the corpse was lowered, just as it was, into a deep pit. Then the husband, bidding farewell to all his friends, stretched himself upon another bier, upon which were laid seven little loaves of bread and a pitcher of water, and he also was let down-down-down to the depths of the horrible cavern, and then a stone was laid over the opening, and the melancholy company wended its way back to the city.

You can probably guess that I wasn't a mute observer of these events; for everyone else, it was something they had grown accustomed to since they were young, but I was so horrified that I couldn't help but tell the king how it made me feel.

"The unusual practice of burying the living beside the dead exists in your dominions, Sir, and I can't begin to tell you how amazed I am. I have never before encountered such an abominable and terrible law in all my travels."

He responded, "What would you have, Sindbad?" "The law applies to everyone. If the Queen were the first to pass away, I ought to be buried next to her."

But, Your Majesty, may I dare to inquire as to whether foreigners are also subject to this law?

They are not an exception to the rule if they got married in the nation, the king said with a smile in what I could only describe as a rather callous attitude.

When I heard this I went home much cast down, and from that time forward my mind was never easy. If only my wife's little finger ached I fancied she was going to die, and sure enough before very long she fell ill and in a few days breathed her last. My dismay was great, for it seemed to me that to be buried alive was even a worse fate than to be devoured by cannibals, nevertheless, there was no escape. The body of my wife, arrayed in her richest robes and decked with all her jewels, was laid upon the bier. I followed it, and after me came a great procession, headed by the king and all his nobles, and in this order, we reached the fatal mountain, which was one of a lofty chain bordering the sea.

Here I made one more frantic effort to excite the pity of the king and those who stood by, hoping to save myself even at this last moment, but it was of no avail. No one spoke to me, they even appeared to hasten over their dreadful task, and I speedily found myself descending into the gloomy pit, with my seven loaves and pitcher of water beside me. Almost before I reached the bottom the stone was rolled into its place above my head, and I was left to my fate. A feeble ray of light shone into the cavern through some chink, and when I dared to look about me I could see that I was in a vast vault, bestrewn with bones and bodies of the dead. I even fancied that I heard the expiring sighs of those who, like myself, had come into this dismal place alive. All in vain did I shriek aloud with rage and despair, reproaching myself for the love of gain and adventure which had brought me to such a pass, but at length, growing calmer, I took up my bread and water, and wrapping my face in my mantle I groped my way towards the end of the cavern, where the air was fresher.

Here I lived in darkness and misery until my provisions were exhausted, but just as I was nearly dead from starvation the rock was rolled away overhead and I saw that a bier was being lowered into the cavern and that the corpse upon it was a man. In a moment my mind was made up, the woman who followed had nothing to expect but a lingering death; I should be doing her a service if I shortened her misery. Therefore when she descended, already insensible from terror, I was ready armed with a huge bone, one blow from which left her dead, and I secured the bread and water which gave me hope of life. Several times did I have recourse to this desperate expedient, and I know not how long I had been a prisoner when one day I fancied that I heard something near me, which breathed loudly. Turning to the place from which the sound came I dimly saw a shadowy form that fled at my movement, squeezing itself through a cranny in the wall. I pursued it as fast as I could and found myself in a narrow crack among the rocks, along which I was just able to force my way. I followed it for what seemed to me many miles, and at last, saw before me a glimmer of light which grew clearer every moment until I emerged upon the sea shore with a joy that I cannot describe. When I was sure that I was not dreaming, I realized that it was doubtless some little animal that had found its way into the cavern from the sea, and when disturbed had fled, showing me a means of escape that I could never have discovered for myself. I hastily surveyed my surroundings and saw that I was safe from all pursuit from the town.

The mountains sloped sheer down to the sea, and there was no road across them. Being assured of this I returned to the cavern and amassed a rich treasure of diamonds, rubies, emeralds, and jewels of all kinds which strewed the ground. These I made up into bales, and stored them into a safe place upon the beach, and then waited hopefully for the passing of a ship. I had looked out for two days, however, before a single sail appeared, so it was with much delight that I, at last, saw a vessel not very far from the shore, and by waving my arms and uttering loud cries succeeded in attracting the attention of her crew. A boat was sent off to me, and in answer to the questions of the sailors as to how I came to be in such a plight, I replied that I had been shipwrecked two days before, but had managed to scramble ashore with the bales which I pointed out to them. Luckily for me, they believed my story, and without even looking at the place where they found me, took up my bundles, and rowed me back to the ship. Once on board, I soon saw that the captain was too much occupied with the difficulties of navigation to pay much heed to me, though he generously made me welcome, and would not even accept the jewels with which I offered to pay my passage. Our voyage was prosperous, and after visiting many lands, and collecting in each place a great store of goodly merchandise, I found myself at last in Bagdad once more with unheard of riches of every description. Again I gave large sums of money to the poor, and enriched all the mosques in the city, after which I gave myself up to my friends and relations, with whom I passed my time in feasting and merriment.

At this point, Sindbad paused, and all of his listeners exclaimed that his fourth voyage's exploits had delighted them more than anything they had previously heard. They then left, followed by Hindbad, who had been given 100 sequins once more and had been asked to return the following day to tell the tale of the fifth voyage.

Once everyone had eaten and drunk everything that had been placed in front of them, Sindbad started telling his story.

Voyage No. 5

Even after everything I had been through, I was unable to settle for a simple life. My desire for change and adventure grew as I quickly became weary of its joys. So I set off once more, but this time I had the ship that I had constructed and outfitted at the closest seaport. Since I didn't plan on carrying enough goods for a full load, I invited several merchants from many countries to join me in my quest to be free to call at whatever port I pleased, at my own pace. We started with the first favorable breeze, and after a protracted journey across the ocean, we arrived at a mysterious island that turned out to be uninhabited. We decided to explore it, though and were not far along when we came across a roc's egg that was just as enormous as the one I had previously seen and was very close to hatching because the juvenile bird's beak had already penetrated the shell. Despite everything I said to try and discourage them, the businessmen who were with me pounced on it with their hatchets, shattering the shell and killing the juvenile roc. They started a fire on the ground, chopped up pieces of the bird, and started roasting them while I watched in shock.

Scarcely had they finished their ill-omened repast when the air above us was darkened by two mighty shadows? The captain of my ship, knowing by experience what this meant, cried out to us that the parent birds were coming, and urged us to get on board with all speed. This we did, and the sails were hoisted, but before we had made any way the rocs reached their despoiled nest and hovered about it, uttering frightful cries when they discovered the mangled remains of their young one. For a moment we lost sight of them, and were flattering ourselves that we had escaped when they reappeared and soared into the air directly over our vessel, and we saw that each held in its claws an immense rock ready to crush us. There was a moment of breathless suspense, then one bird loosed its hold and the huge block of stone hurtled through the air, but thanks to the presence of mind of the helmsman, who turned our ship violently in another direction, it fell into the sea close beside us, cleaving it asunder till we could nearly see the bottom. We had hardly time to draw a breath of relief before the other rock fell with a mighty crash right amid our luckless vessel, smashing it into a thousand fragments, and crushing, or hurling it into the sea, passengers and crew. I went down with the rest but had the good fortune to rise unhurt, and by holding on to a piece of driftwood with one hand and swimming with the other I kept myself afloat and was presently washed up by the tide onto an island. Its shores were steep and rocky, but I scrambled up safely and threw myself down to rest upon the green turf.

When I had somewhat recovered I began to examine the spot in which I found myself, and truly it seemed to me that I had reached a garden of delights. There were trees everywhere, and they were laden with flowers and fruit, while a crystal stream wandered in and out under their shadow. When night came I slept sweetly in a cozy nook, though the remembrance that I was alone in a strange land made me sometimes start up and look around me in alarm, and then I wished heartily that I had stayed at home at ease. However, the morning sunlight restored my courage, and

I once more wandered among the trees, but always with some anxiety as to what I might see next. I had penetrated some distance into the island when I saw an old man bent and feeble sitting upon the river bank, and at first, I took him to be some ship-wrecked mariner like myself. Going up to him I greeted him in a friendly way, but he only nodded his head at me in reply. I then asked what he did there, and he made signs to me that he wished to get across the river to gather some fruit, and seemed to beg me to carry him on my back. Pitying his age and feebleness, I took him up, and wading across the stream I bent down that he might more easily reach the bank, and bade him get down. But instead of allowing himself to be set upon his feet (even now it makes me laugh to think of it!), this creature who had seemed to me so decrepit leaped nimbly upon my shoulders, and hooking his legs round my neck gripped me so tightly that I was well-nigh choked, and so overcome with terror that I fell insensible to the ground. When I recovered my enemy was still in his place, though he had released his hold enough to allow me breathing space, and seeing me revive he prodded me adroitly first with one foot and then with the other until I was forced to get up and stagger about with him under the trees while he gathered and ate the choicest fruits. This went on all day, and even at night, when I threw myself down half dead with weariness, the terrible old man held on tight to my neck, nor did he fail to greet the first glimmer of morning light by drumming upon me with his heels, until I perforce awoke and resumed my dreary march with rage and bitterness in my heart.

It happened one day that I passed a tree under which lay several dry gourds, and catching one up I amused myself with scooping out its contents and pressing into it the juice of several bunches of grapes that hung from every bush.

When it was full I left it propped in the fork of a tree, and a few days later, carrying the hateful old man that way, I snatched at my gourd as I passed it and had the satisfaction of a draught of excellent wine so good and refreshing that I even forgot my detestable burden, and began to sing and caper.

The old monster was not slow to perceive the effect which my draught had produced and that I carried him more lightly than usual, so he stretched out his skinny hand and seizing the gourd first tasted its contents cautiously, then drained them to the very last drop. The wine was strong and the gourd capacious, so he also began to sing after a fashion, and soon I had the delight of feeling the iron grip of his goblin legs unclasp, and with one vigorous effort, I threw him to the ground, from which he never moved again. I was so rejoiced to have at last got rid of this uncanny old man that I ran leaping and bounding down to the sea shore, where, by the greatest good luck, I met with some mariners who had anchored off the island to enjoy the delicious fruits, and to renew their supply of water.

They heard the story of my escape with amazement, saying, "You fell into the hands of the Old Man of the Sea, and it is a mercy that he did not strangle you as he has everyone else upon whose shoulders he has managed to perch himself. This island is well known as the scene of his evil deeds, and no merchant or sailor who lands upon it cares to stray far away from his comrades." After we had talked for a while they took me back with them on board their ship, where the captain received me kindly, and we soon set sail, and after several days reached a large and prosperous-looking town where all the houses were built of stone. Here we anchored, and one of the merchants, who had been very friendly to me on the way, took me ashore with him and showed me a lodging set apart for strange merchants. He then provided me with a large sack and pointed out to me a party of others equipped in like manner.

"Go with them," said he, "and do as they do, but beware of losing sight of them, for if you strayed your life would be in danger."

With that, he supplied me with provisions and bade me farewell, and I set out with my new companions. I soon learned that the object of our expedition was to fill our sacks with cocoanuts, but when at length I saw the trees and noted their immense height and the slippery smoothness of their slender trunks, I did not at all understand how we were to do it. The crowns of the cocoa palms were all alive with monkeys, big and little, which skipped from one to the other with surprising agility, seeming to be curious about us and disturbed at our appearance, and I was at first surprised when my companions after collecting stones began to throw them at the living creatures, which seemed to me quite harmless. But very soon I saw the reason for it and joined them heartily, for the monkeys, annoyed and wishing to pay us back in our coin, began to tear the nuts from the trees and cast them at us with angry and spiteful gestures so that after very little labor our sacks were filled with the fruit which we could not otherwise have obtained.

As soon as we had as many as we could carry we went back to the town, where my friend bought my share and advised me to continue the same occupation until I had earned money enough to carry me to my own country. This I did, and before long had amassed a considerable sum. Just then I heard that there was a trading ship ready to sail, and taking leave of my friend I went on board, carrying with me a goodly store of cocoanuts; and we sailed first to the islands where the pepper grows, then to Comair where the best aloes wood is found, and where men drink no wine by an unalterable law. Here I exchanged my nuts for pepper and good aloe wood and went a-fishing for pearls with some of the other merchants, and my divers were so lucky that very soon I had an immense number, and those very large and perfect. With all these treasures I came joyfully back to Bagdad, where I disposed of them for large sums of money, of which I did not fail as before to give the tenth part to the poor, and after that, I rested from my labors and comforted myself with all the pleasures that my riches could give me.

After concluding his tale in this manner, Sindbad gave the order to give Hindbad 100 sequins, and the guests departed. However, following the feast the following day, Sindbad began to describe his sixth voyage as follows.

The Sixth Voyage

You must find it amazing that, after experiencing shipwreck and previously unheard-of dangers five times, I could once more tempt fate and take a chance on a new difficulty. When I think back, I'm even startled by myself. However, it seems that wandering was part of my destiny since, after a year of rest, I prepared to embark on my sixth journey against the pleas of my friends and family, who tried their best to keep me at home. I traveled quite a distance by land instead of via the Persian Gulf, and I eventually boarded a ship from a far-off port in India with a captain who intended to do a long journey. And in fact, he did so because we encountered inclement weather that entirely changed our route, leaving neither the captain nor the pilot aware of our location or direction for several days. We had little cause for celebration when they finally found us because the captain stated that we were in the most hazardous location on the entire ocean and had been caught in a current that was currently carrying us to our doom, flinging his turban to the deck and rending his beard.

Too true to be true! Despite the sailors' best efforts, we were propelled quickly towards the base of a mountain that rose sheer out of the water, where our ship was smashed to bits on the rocks. However, not before we had managed to scramble onshore and bring the most valuable items with us. The skipper remarked to us once we had completed this:

Since no shipwrecked mariner has ever returned from this terrible site, we might as well start digging our graves right away.

This speech greatly demoralized us, and we started to mourn our unfortunate circumstances.

The mountain formed the seaward boundary of a large island, and the narrow strip of rocky shore upon which we stood was strewn with the wreckage of a thousand gallant ships, while the bones of the luckless mariners shone white in the sunshine, and we shuddered to think how soon our own would be added to the heap. All around, too, lay vast quantities of the costliest merchandise and treasures were heaped in every cranny of the rocks, but all these things only added to the desolation of the scene. It struck me as a very strange thing that a river of clear fresh water, which gushed out from the mountain not far from where we stood, instead of flowing into the sea as rivers generally do turn off sharply, and flowed out of sight under a natural archway of rock, and when I went to examine it more closely I found that inside the cave the walls were thick with diamonds, and rubies, and masses of crystal, and the floor was strewn with ambergris. Here, then, upon this desolate shore, we abandoned ourselves to our fate, for there was no possibility of scaling the mountain, and if a ship had appeared it could only have shared our doom. The first thing our captain did was to divide equally amongst us all the food we possessed, and then the length of each man's life depended on the time he could make his portion last. I could live upon very little.

Nevertheless, by the time I had buried the last of my companions my stock of provisions was so small that I hardly thought I should live long enough to dig my own grave, which I set about doing, while I regretted bitterly the roving disposition which was always bringing me into such straits, and thought longingly of all the comfort and luxury that I had left. But luckily for me, the fancy took me to stand once more beside the river where it plunged out of sight into the depths of the cavern, and as I did so an idea struck me. This river which hid underground doubtless emerged again at some distant spot. Why should I not build a raft and trust myself to its swiftly flowing waters? If I perished before I could reach the light of day once more I should be no worse off than I was now, for death stared me in the face, while there was always the possibility that, as I was born under a lucky star, I might find myself safe and sound in some desirable land. I decided at any rate to risk it, and speedily built myself a stout raft of driftwood with strong cords, of which enough and to spare lay strewn upon the beach. I then made up many packages of rubies, emeralds, rock crystal, ambergris, and precious stuff, and bound them upon my raft, being careful to preserve the balance, and then I seated myself upon it, having two small oars that I had fashioned laid ready to my hand, and loosed the cord which held it to the bank. Once out in the current, my raft flew swiftly under the gloomy archway, and I found myself in total darkness, carried smoothly forward by the rapid river. On I went as it seemed to me for many nights and days. Once the channel became so small that I had a narrow escape from being crushed against the rocky roof, and after that, I took the precaution of lying flat upon my precious bales. Though I only ate what was necessary to keep myself alive, the inevitable moment came when, after swallowing my last morsel of food, I began to wonder if I must after all die of hunger. Then, worn out with anxiety and fatigue, I fell into a deep sleep, and when I again opened my eyes I was once more in the light of day; a beautiful country lay before me, and my raft, which was tied to the river bank, was surrounded by friendly looking black men. I rose and saluted them, and they spoke to me in return, but I could not understand a word of their language. Feeling perfectly bewildered by my sudden return to life and light, I murmured to myself in Arabic, "Close thine eyes, and while thou sleepest Heaven will change thy fortune from evil to good."

Then a local who spoke this tongue stepped up and said:

"Be not alarmed to see us, my brother; this is our territory. We came to the river to gather water when we saw your raft floating down it; one of us swam out and carried you to the shore. Tell us now where you came from and where you were headed by that risky route while we have been waiting for your awakening."

I replied that nothing would please me better than to tell them, but that I was starving, and would fain eat something first. I was soon supplied with all I needed, and having satisfied my hunger I told them faithfully all that had befallen me. They were lost in wonder at my tale when it was interpreted to them and said that adventures so surprising must be related to their king only by the man to whom they had happened. So, procuring a horse, they mounted me upon it, and we set out, followed by several strong men carrying my raft just as it was upon their shoulders. In this order we marched into the city of Serendib, where the natives presented me to their king, whom I saluted in the Indian fashion, prostrating myself at his feet and kissing the ground; but the monarch bade me rise and sit beside him, asking first what was my name.

I responded, "I am Sindbad, sometimes known as 'the Sailor,' because I have traveled widely over many seas.

And how did you end up here? the king inquired.

I told him about my exploits while keeping nothing secret, and he was so surprised and delighted that he had them recorded in gold letters and kept in the kingdom's archives.

Presently my raft was brought in and the bales opened in his presence, and the king declared that in all his treasury there were no such rubies and emeralds as those which lay in great heaps before him. Seeing that he looked at them with interest, I ventured to say that I and all that I had were at his disposal, but he answered me smiling:

"Nay, Sindbad. Heaven forbid that I should covet your riches; I will rather add to them, for I desire that you shall not leave my kingdom without some tokens of my goodwill." He then commanded his officers to provide me with suitable lodging at his expense and sent slaves to wait upon me and carry my raft and my bales to my new dwelling place. You may imagine that I praised his generosity and gave him thanks, nor did I fail to present myself daily in his audience chamber, and for the rest of my time, I amused myself in seeing all that was most worthy of attention in the city. The island of Serendib is situated on the equinoctial line, the days and nights there are of equal length. The chief city is placed at the end of a beautiful valley, formed by the highest mountain in the world, which is in the middle of the island. I had the curiosity to ascend to its very summit, for this was the place to which Adam was banished out of Paradise. Here are found rubies and many precious things, and rare plants grow abundantly, with cedar trees and cocoa palms. On the seashore and at the mouths of the rivers the divers seek pearls, and in some valleys diamonds are plentiful. After many days I petitioned the king that I might return to my own country, to which he graciously consented. Moreover, he loaded me with rich gifts, and when I went to take leave of him he entrusted me with a royal present and a letter to the Commander of the Faithful, our sovereign lord, saying, "I pray you to give these to the Caliph Haroun al Raschid and assure him of my friendship."

I accepted the charge respectfully and soon embarked upon the vessel that the king himself had chosen for me. The king's letter was written in blue characters upon a rare and precious skin of yellowish color, and these were the words of it: "The King of the Indies, before whom walk a thousand elephants, who lives in a palace, of which the roof blazes with a hundred thousand rubies, and whose treasure house contains twenty thousand diamond crowns, to the Caliph Haroun al Raschid sends greeting. Though the offering we present to you is unworthy of your notice, we pray you to accept it as a mark of the esteem and friendship which we cherish for you, and of which we gladly send you this token, and we ask of you a like regard if you deem us worthy of it. Adieu, brother."

The present consisted of a vase carved from a single ruby, six inches high and as thick as my finger; this was filled with the choicest pearls, large, and of perfect shape and luster; secondly, a huge snake skin, with scales as large as a sequin, which would preserve from sickness those who slept upon it. Then quantities of aloes wood, camphor, and pistachio nuts; and lastly, a beautiful slave girl, whose robes glittered with precious stones.

After a lengthy and successful voyage, we arrived at Balsora. I hurried to Bagdad and, armed with the king's letter and the treasure, I presented myself at the palace gate. The lovely slave and numerous members of my own family also arrived with me.

As soon as I announced my mission, I was led into the presence of the Caliph. After bowing respectfully, I delivered him the letter and the present from the king. After he had a chance to inspect both, he then asked me if the Prince of Serendib was as wealthy and powerful as he had claimed to be.

"Commander of the Faithful," I replied, again bowing humbly before him, "I can assure your Majesty that he has in no way exaggerated his wealth and grandeur. Nothing can equal the magnificence of his palace. When he goes abroad his throne is prepared upon the back of an elephant, and on either side of him ride his ministers, his favorites, and courtiers. On his elephant's neck sits an officer, his golden lance in his hand, and behind him stands another bearing a pillar of gold, at the top of which is an emerald as long as my hand. A thousand men in cloth of gold, mounted upon richly caparisoned elephants, go before him, and as the procession moves onward the officer who guides his elephant cries aloud, `Behold the mighty monarch, the powerful and valiant Sultan of the Indies, whose palace is covered with a hundred thousand rubies, who possesses twenty thousand diamond crowns. Behold a monarch greater than Solomon and Mirage in all their glory!'"

The person standing in front of the throne then responds, "This monarch, so great and powerful, must die, must die, must die!"

And the first begins chanting once more, "All praise to Him who lives for evermore."

Furthermore, my lord, Serendib does not require a judge because the people come directly to the monarch to seek justice.

My report met with the Caliph's complete satisfaction.

"He said, "I determined that the monarch was a wise man from the letter.

He appears to be deserving of his people, and they of him."

Saying thus, he sent me on my way bearing valuable gifts, and I went home in peace.

After Sindbad finished speaking, his visitors left. Sindbad had been given 100 sequins before they left, but

"I determined that the king was a clever guy based on the letter, he stated.

He looks to be deserving of his people, and they appear to be deserving of him."

With that, he sent me off with a bounty of gifts, and I went back to my own home in peace.

After Sindbad finished speaking, his guests left after Hindbad collected 100 sequins, but they all came back the following day to hear Sindbad's account of the seventh voyage.

Seventh and Final Journey

I was pretty sure I wouldn't travel to sea again after my sixth voyage. I had taken enough chances and was now of an age to appreciate a tranquil existence. I merely wanted to pass away quietly. But one day, while I was hosting a lot of my friends, I received word that a caliph's officer wanted to talk with me. When he was admitted, he asked me to follow him into Haroun al Raschid's presence, so I did what he asked. The Caliph said after I had saluted him:

"I sent for you because I need your help, Sindbad. In exchange for his message of friendliness, I have chosen you to deliver a letter and a gift to the King of Serendib."

The Caliph's commandment struck me like a bolt of lightning.

"I said, "Commander of the Faithful, I am willing to do all that your Majesty commands, but I respectfully pray you to keep in mind that I am profoundly saddened by the unprecedented miseries I have experienced.
I've vowed never to leave Bagdad again."

After that, I calmly listened to him as I delivered a lengthy explanation of some of my craziest adventures.

"I admit," said he, "that you have indeed had some extraordinary experiences, but I do not see why they should hinder you from doing as I wish. You have only to go straight to Serendib and give my message, then you are free to come back and do as you will. But go you must; my honor and dignity demand it."V

As there was no assistance available, I announced that I was willing to obey. The Caliph, ecstatic that he had gotten his way, then offered me a thousand sequins to cover the costs of the journey. As soon as I was prepared to begin, I boarded the Balsora and traveled swiftly and safely to Serendib while carrying the message and the gift. When I revealed my mission here, I was welcomed and escorted into the king's presence, where he joyfully greeted me.

He exclaimed, "Welcome, Sindbad. "I have often thought of you and am glad to meet you again."

After thanking him for the honor that he did me, I displayed the Caliph's gifts. First a bed with complete hangings all cloth of gold, which cost a thousand sequins, and another like to it of crimson stuff. Fifty robes of rich embroidery, a hundred of the finest white linen from Cairo, Suez, Cufa, and Alexandria. Then more beds of different fashion, an agate vase carved with the figure of a man aiming an arrow at a lion, and finally a costly table, which had once belonged to King Solomon. The King of Serendib received with satisfaction the assurance of the Caliph's friendliness toward him, and now my task being accomplished I was anxious to depart, but it was some time before the king would think of letting me go. At last, however, he dismissed me with many presents, and I lost no time in going on board a ship, which sailed at once, and for four days all went well. On the fifth day, we had the misfortune to fall in with pirates, who seized our vessel, killing all who resisted, and making prisoners of those who were prudent enough to submit at once, of whom I was one. When they had despoiled us of all we possessed, they forced us to put on vile raiment, and sailing to a distant island there sold us for slaves. I fell into the hands of a rich merchant, who took me home with him, and clothed and fed me well, and after some days sent for me and questioned me as to what I could do.

I said that I didn't know any commerce because I was a wealthy merchant who had been kidnapped by pirates.

Tell me, can you shoot a bow, he demanded.

I retorted that this was one of my childhood interests and that I was sure that with practice, I would regain my skill.

Upon this, he provided me with a bow and arrows, and mounting me with him upon his elephant took the way to a vast forest that lay far from the town. When we had reached the wildest part of it we stopped, and my master said to me:

"This forest swarms with elephants. Hide in this great tree, and shoot at all that pass you. When you have succeeded in killing one come and tell me."

So saying he gave me a supply of food, and returned to the town, and I perched myself high up in the tree and kept watch. That night I saw nothing, but just after sunrise the next morning a large herd of elephants came crashing and trampling by. I lost no time in letting fly several arrows, and at last one of the great animals fell to the ground dead, and the others retreated, leaving me free to come down from my hiding place and run back to tell my master of my success, for which I was praised and regaled with good things. Then we went back to the forest together and dug a mighty trench in which we buried the elephant I had killed so that when it became a skeleton my master might return and secure its tusks.

For two months I hunted thus, and no day passed without my securing, an elephant. Of course, I did not always station myself in the same tree, but sometimes in one place, sometimes in another. One morning as I watched the coming of the elephants I was surprised to see that, instead of passing the tree I was in, as they usually did, they paused, and surrounded it, trumpeting horribly, and shaking the very ground with their heavy tread, and when I saw that their eyes were fixed upon me I was terrified, and my arrows dropped from my trembling hand. I had indeed good reason for my terror when, an instant later, the largest of the animals wound his trunk round the stem of my tree, and with one mighty effort tore it up by the roots, bringing me to the ground entangled in its branches. I thought now that my last hour was surely come; but the huge creature, picking me up gently enough, set me upon its back, where I clung more dead than alive, and followed by the whole herd turned and crashed off into the dense forest. It seemed to me a long time before I was once more set upon my feet by the elephant, and I stood as if in a dream watching the herd, which turned and trampled off in another direction and were soon hidden in the dense underwood. Then, recovering myself, I looked about me and found that I was standing upon the side of a great hill, strewn as far as I could see on either hand with bones and tusks of elephants. "This then must be the elephants' burying place," I said to myself, "and they must have brought me here that I might cease to persecute them, seeing that I want nothing but their tusks, and here lie more than I could carry away in a lifetime."

Whereupon I turned and made for the city as fast as I could go, not seeing a single elephant by the way, which convinced me that they had retired deeper into the forest to leave the way open to the Ivory Hill, and I did not know how sufficiently to admire their sagacity. After a day and a night, I reached my master's house and was received by him with joyful surprise.

"Poor Sindbad, I was wondering what might have happened to you," he wept. I was afraid I would never see you again when I arrived at the forest and saw the tree had just been uprooted and the arrows were lying alongside it. Please explain how you managed to survive."

He was delighted to learn that I had told him nothing but the truth when we visited Ivory Hill the following day after I had quickly allayed his curiosity. He remarked this while we were returning to the city after packing our elephant with all of its tusks.

"My brother--since I can no longer treat as a slave one who has enriched me thus--take your liberty and may Heaven prosper you. I will no longer conceal from you that these wild elephants have killed a number of our slaves every year. No matter what good advice we gave them, they were caught sooner or later. You alone have escaped the wiles of these animals, therefore you must be under the special protection of Heaven. Now through you, the whole town will be enriched without further loss of life, therefore you shall not only receive your liberty, but I will also bestow a fortune upon you."

I then responded, "Thank you, Master, and best wishes for further success.
I merely beg for the freedom to go back to my nation for myself."

The monsoon will soon bring the ivory ships here, so it's okay, he said. "I'll send you on your way with something to cover your voyage," he said.

So I stayed with him till the time of the monsoon, and every day we added to our store of ivory till all his warehouses were overflowing with it. By this time the other merchants knew the secret, but there was enough and to spare for all. When the ships, at last, arrived my master himself chose the one in which I was to sail and put on board for me a great store of choice provisions, also ivory in abundance, and all the costliest curiosities of the country, for which I could not thank him enough, and so we parted. I left the ship at the first port we came to, not feeling at ease upon the sea after all that had happened to me because of it, and having disposed of my ivory for much gold, and bought many rare and costly presents, I loaded my pack animals, and joined a caravan of merchants. Our journey was long and tedious, but I bore it patiently, reflecting that at least I had not to fear tempests, pirates, serpents, nor any of the other perils from which I had suffered before, and at length we reached Bagdad. My first care was to present myself before the Caliph and give him an account of my embassy. He assured me that my long absence had disquieted him much, but he had nevertheless hoped for the best. As to my adventure among the elephants he heard it with amazement, declaring that he could not have believed it had not my truthfulness been well known to him.

By his orders, this story and the others I had told him were written by his scribes in letters of gold and laid up among his treasures. I took my leave of him, well satisfied with the honors and rewards he bestowed upon me; and since that time I have rested from my labors, and given myself up wholly to my family and my friends.

After completing the account of his seventh and final journey, Sindbad turned to Hindbad and added:

"Now tell me, my buddy, what do you think? Do you know of anyone who has endured more suffering or had more narrow escapes than I have?
Is it not just fair that I should now live a life of comfort and peace?"

Printed by Libri Plureos GmbH in Hamburg, Germany

9 798888 052570